MORRIS
IS A COWBOY

a Policeman and a Baby Sitter

Story and pictures by
B. WISEMAN

An I CAN READ Book

HARPER & ROW, PUBLISHERS
NEW YORK, EVANSTON, AND LONDON

CONTENTS

MORRIS
IS A COWBOY

a Policeman and a Baby Sitter

MORRIS IS A POLICEMAN

Morris the Moose

wanted to be a policeman.

He went to see

the chief of police.

"Can I be a policeman?" Morris asked.
The chief laughed. "You're a MOOSE,
but I'll let you try!"

He gave Morris

a police coat and hat,

a badge and a whistle.

Morris put the hat on his antler.

The chief said,

"No! Put it on your head!"

Morris put the hat on his head.

He hung the whistle on his antler!

Then he went to work.

He held up his hoof
and whistled, "STOP!"
He waved his hoof
and whistled, "GO!"
He whistled all day long.

The next morning it rained.

Morris had to wear a raincoat.

The rain left big puddles.

Morris carried the children

across the puddles.

They didn't get wet feet.

The chief gave Morris

a police horse to ride.

The horse said,

"Gee, you're a MOOSE!"

16

"Oh, yes," Morris said,

"and I'm heavy!

I'll walk

so you won't get tired."

They walked

to the fruit store.

The fruit man

gave them each an apple.

Then they walked

to the park.

The horse talked to the zebra.

Morris said, "Hello,"

to the moose.

Some people fed Morris peanuts.

He said, "You're very nice to policemen."

Morris said, "Keep off the grass."

He kept it clean.

He liked to eat clean grass!

Morris and the horse

saw a pony giving rides.

The moose said,

"I'll bet he never gets a rest!"

Morris and the horse

gave the children rides.

The pony took a rest!

A little boy yelled,

"Yipppeee!!! I'm a COWBOY!"

"What's that?" Morris asked.

The boy told Morris about cowboys.

About cowboys, and cows and the West.

"I'm going West!" Morris said.

"It sounds like fun!"

MORRIS IS A COWBOY

Morris was in a hurry.

He ran all the way.

He was out of breath

when he got to the West.

27

Morris saw two cowboys.

He said,

"I want to be a cowboy, too!"

They laughed.

"You're a MOOSE,

but we'll let you try!"

They gave Morris

a cowboy suit and hat,

and a big white cowboy horse.

When Morris got on,

the horse bucked.

Morris yelled, "Yipppeee!!!"

Morris said, "Would you like a ride?"

And the horse got on Morris.

Morris bucked as hard as he could.

The horse yelled, "Yippppeeee!!"

Then Morris tried to lasso a cow.

He swung the lasso around his head.

But his antlers got in the way!

Morris lassoed himself!

That night
Morris tried
to sing
the cows to sleep.
But a moose
sounds like
a horn on a car!
The cows
couldn't sleep!
The horses
put a hoof
in each ear!

Morris sang so much HE got tired.

He fell asleep!

Then so did the horses and cows.

In the morning the cowboys washed.

Morris was the last to finish.

He had more face to wash!

An Indian saw Morris.

He said, "How."

The moose laughed.

"Ha, ha! You have funny antlers!"

The Indian laughed.

"You have funny feathers

on your head!"

The Indian took Morris

to the Indian camp.

The moose looked around.

"Ha, ha! You live

in big ice-cream cones!"

When it got late,

Morris left.

On his way back

to the cowboys

he saw a moose.

He ran to say, "Hello."

But it wasn't a moose.

It was a cactus!

Morris said, "Hello!" anyway.

"It's fun to talk!" Morris laughed.
"I'll go to town and get a job
with lots of talking!"

MORRIS IS A BABY SITTER

When Morris got to town, he saw a sign.

It said, BABY SITTER WANTED.

Morris said, "That's a good job for me.

I could tell stories!"

He knocked on the door.

A lady opened it and he said,

"I want to be a baby sitter!"

The lady laughed.

"You're a MOOSE, but I'll let you try!

Come in."

"This is our boy Herbert."

Morris said, "Hello, Herbert."

Herbert asked, "Are you a cowboy?"

"I was," Morris said. "Long ago!"

Then the lady and her husband left.

Morris and Herbert waved good-bye.

Morris said, "Herbert,

it's time to go to bed.

Put on your pajamas.

Can you do that alone?"

Herbert said, "Yes."

But Morris tried

to help him anyway.

He was in a hurry.

He wanted

to tell Herbert

a story.

Morris put the pants on Herbert's head!

"Oh, dear," Morris cried.

"You're standing upside down!"

Herbert put the pajamas on himself.

He got into bed and said,

"Now tell me a story.

Tell me about Little Red Riding Hood!"

"Well," Morris began, "there was once a little boy named . . ."

"NO!" Herbert yelled. "It was a GIRL!"

"Oh, yes," Morris said, "there was once a little girl named Red Riding Hood! Well, Herbert, this little girl went to visit her grandfather. . . ."

Herbert shook his head. "NO!
You mean her grandMOTHER!"

"Oh, yes, her grandmother!"

Morris laughed.

"Well, one day this little boy

went to visit his grandmother. . . ."

Herbert yelled, "IT WAS A GIRL!"

"I know grandmothers are girls!"
Morris said.

Herbert shook his head again.

"NO! The little BOY was a GIRL!"

"How can a little boy be a girl?"
Morris asked.

Herbert sighed. "In the STORY
she was a girl!"

"Oh, all right . . ." Morris said.
And then he went on.

"Well, this little GIRL

who was a grandMOTHER

visited a little BOY. . . ."

"NO! NO! NO!" Herbert cried.

"A little girl named Red Riding Hood

visited her grandmother!"

"Oh, yes," Morris said.

"Well, she got there

and found a fox in the bed."

"The FOX was a WOLF!"

Herbert yelled.

"How can a fox be a wolf?"

Morris asked.

Herbert said, "In the STORY

it was a wolf!

You see, here's how it happened. . . .

This wolf made believe

HE was the grandmother. . . ."

Morris said, "And then?"

"Then," Herbert went on, "the little girl named Red Riding Hood went to visit her grandmother. When she saw the wolf she said, 'Grandma, what big eyes you have!'"

Morris asked, "And what did the wolf say?"

Herbert told him.

He told him the whole story.

When he was done Morris said,

"How did you like the story

I just told you?"

"The story YOU told ME?"

Herbert laughed.

"Yes!" Morris said. "The one about
Little Green Riding Hood!
Did you like it?"

"It was a good story." Herbert sighed.
"I like stories about foxes."

Then Herbert yawned. He was tired.

When Herbert's parents came home

he was asleep.

They said, "You're a good baby sitter.

Will you baby sit again?"

Morris said, "Sure!

I know lots of stories

to tell Herbert.

I'll tell him about

The Four Little Pigs,

Jack and Bill,

The Pretty Duckling,

and Jack and the Corn-Stalk!"

The parents laughed

and waved good-bye.

Morris said, "Now I think

I'll go to sleep!"

He lay down under a tree.

Just before he closed his eyes he said,

"Let's see—was that story about

FOUR little pigs, or FIVE?"